PANCAKES AND PLEAS

Day and Night Diner, Book 1

GRETCHEN ALLEN

Summer Prescott Books Publishing

CHAPTER ONE

The Day and Night Diner was full of life even before the sun rose. For Josslyn Rockwell, every morning began the same way. She'd arrive at five-forty-five, just before her shift began, taking over the responsibilities of the overnight waitress, Becky. Joss would make sure that there was some extra coffee brewed, that the tables were cleared and set, and that her boss, Luke, wasn't napping in his car. Like she always said, just another normal day.

"How was last night?" Joss asked, emptying a bag of coffee grounds into a filter.

"Pretty decent actually. A huge bus came through full of cheerleaders that were on their way to a competition or something. They came in at like, three and every single one of them ate something, and man, did they eat well. They tipped well, too." Becky grinned.

"Awesome!" she exclaimed, high-fiving her coworker.

"Do you want me to stay for a little while until you get situated?" Becky asked.

Joss looked around the diner. She saw a few people, but most of the tables were empty. That's how it usually was until exactly six o'clock hit.

"I'm probably okay. Where's Luke?" Joss asked, portioning out some butter cups for the inevitable morning rush.

"Good question. He should be around here some-where. He didn't come in until about five, mumbled something about paperwork, and I haven't seen him since. Luckily we've only had a few customers." Becky poured her tip jar into her purse, coins and all.

"So, you did all the cooking, cleaning and serving? Hopefully that's not a tell of how my day will go." Joss sighed.

"Garth was here most of the night cooking." Becky shrugged and hoisted her purse over her shoulder.

"Ya know you can cash your tips in here, right?" Joss asked.

"I know. I just like it better this way. Makes me feel like I always have money on hand. Just reach in and see what I come up with."

"Weirdo. You're gonna have a stiff neck carrying that heavy thing around all day." Joss shook her head and set out a few coffee mugs on the counter.

Just as Becky walked into the kitchen so she could leave out the back door, Luke came out of his office grumbling, and two of her regular customers came in through the front door.

"Joss." Luke gave a nod and brushed past her in a haze.

Luke Prior was a great cook, a good man, an okay business owner, and a barely passable boss. He opened the Day and Night Diner twenty-five years previous and had done very well for himself over the years. The diner was well-known and well-loved by just about everyone in the quaint little town of Lemon Bay. Open twenty-four hours a day, seven

3

days a week, the diner offered something for everyone. Luke took special care of police officers, veterans, senior citizens, and town employees. Like Joss always said, he was a great cook and a good man, the rest left something to be desired.

"Morning, Jack!" Joss greeted one of her regulars. She took the newspaper from him, and gestured for him to have a seat at his regular table where his coffee sat waiting for him.

"How goes it?" Jack asked. "I'll have my bagel this morning, thanks."

"All is well in my corner of the world. Thanks for asking. Blueberry bagel grilled, coming right up." Their interaction was the same every morning.

"Joss. Hello," Hazel Hadley said quietly, heading to her favorite table.

"Hi, Miss Hazel. Having your usual today?"

"Please. And if you don't mind passing me the obituaries..." Hazel began, eyeing Jack.

Every day was the same with these two. They rarely spoke, and when they did it was because someone else was around and they didn't want to make themselves look awkward. They saved that part for Joss. Jack brought in the newspaper, passed it off to Joss, but always tucked the obituary section in his jacket. She didn't know if he did it because it was his favorite section of the paper, which she hoped not because that was super creepy, or if he did it just to give Hazel a hard time.

Joss chuckled and played along. She poured Hazel her mug of coffee and went over to the counter, pulling apart the newspaper. "Gee. I can't seem to find it. Is there another section you want?"

"Very funny. I'll wait." Hazel gave Jack her best side eye and poured some sugar into her coffee, grumbling away under her breath.

Joss shook her head and looked between the two customers. She couldn't help but notice the sly grin on Jack's face. For what it was worth, it seemed like these two enjoyed their odd friendship.

"I'll go get started on your breakfast," Joss said, talking to both of them.

Coming around the corner and up the two steps

behind the counter, Joss made her way into the kitchen. She wasn't sure why she thought Luke would be in there waiting for an order to cook. Peering out the small window on the kitchen door that led outside to the parking lot, she saw Luke in the front seat of his car, happily puffing away on his trademark cigar.

Of course, she thought to herself. Scolding herself for giving Luke too much credit. If nothing else, she could thank him for abandoning her so often that she was able to learn the ropes of the restaurant business all on her own. Joss could cook and wait tables mid-breakfast rush all by herself. The lunch shift got a little tricky when she was on her own, but more often than not a second waitress was on schedule right before the busiest part of the afternoon began.

Joss pulled out a blueberry bagel from the pantry behind the main kitchen area, slathered it with butter and dropped in on the already warm grill. She took two slices of precooked bacon and one sausage link and placed them on the back of the grill to warm slowly while she worked on Hazel's eggs. She requested them to be "fried perfectly over-medium with absolutely no brown spots, and if the egg is broken, I'll send it back. Along with a slice of sourdough toast, not too light and not too dark". Not only could Joss recite the order word for word but chances were, she could also make it with her eyes closed. Despite everything, she loved her quirky customers, and she loved her job.

CHAPTER TWO

"Twenty-four and twenty-five." Joss counted back the customer's change.

"Thank you. We loved everything and will definitely be back."

Joss had just served a younger couple that she hadn't recognized. When that happened, she always tried hard to make conversation and learn more about the customers. She figured, if they liked the food and the service, and if they are ever in the area again, they will be more likely to come back. It wasn't as though Joss didn't try hard to make everyone happy, but Lemon Bay wasn't exactly a booming metropolis. She'd lived there her entire life and so had pretty much everyone that came in to eat at the diner. Of course, she wanted them to be happy too, but there were plenty of times over the years when they'd had a bad experience and still came back again. It was all about loyalty in a town like Lemon Bay.

"Glad to hear it. We look forward to seeing you again!" Joss waved to the couple as they left. Her wave turning into a hello to the woman that entered moments later.

"Joss. You have to sit. We need to talk." Bridget was frantic, hair all over the place and mascara streaking down her cheeks.

"Are you okay?" Joss asked, coming around to meet Bridget at the counter.

"I don't know." Bridget flopped down on a stool.

"What's going on? Were you crying? Are you hurt?" Joss looked Bridget up and down.

"No. It's not me. It's much worse than being hurt. She was murdered. She was murdered, and I just know it!"

Joss's eyes scanned the diner, noticing the looks they were getting. She didn't want to tell her friend to be quiet if she was serious about murder, but coming to the diner to tell her about it seemed like a poor choice compared to going to the police. Although, sometimes Bridget was known for her theatrics.

"What? Who? And keep your voice down before you cause a scene."

"Danielle Perry," she whispered.

"Danielle? What are you talking about? I just saw her yesterday." Joss thought back to the previous morning when Danielle had come into the diner with some of her coworkers from the hospital after their overnight shift.

"I'm sure you did, but she was found dead last night. Dead. Do you believe it?" Bridget's tears were flowing.

"I'm so sorry," Joss said, trying to console her. Growing up Joss, Bridget, and Danielle had all gone to school together and played on the same basketball team. Bridget and Danielle had stayed close while Joss went her own way over the years.

Joss didn't want to ask the about the gory details while she was at the diner. It was a sensitive situation, and with how upset Bridget was, it would likely make it worse if Joss asked questions.

As if Bridget had read her mind, she spoke. "They found her in the bushes in her backyard, right under her balcony. Her own house. Who does something so awful?" Bridget sniffled.

"Who's they? Who found her?" Joss whispered.

"The cops. They got a call from her parents saying they hadn't heard from her, and asked them to do a welfare check. They ended up getting into her back-yard through the fence gate that was left open and found her there."

"How do you know all of this?" Joss asked.

"Emily told me. I took Ralphie around the block after the dog park, and she was driving by. She stopped me and told me all about it." Bridget wiped her eyes with her sleeve.

"So, it really was murder? Someone killed her?" Joss asked, gently putting her hand on Bridget's shoulder. Emily was Danielle's neighbor, so it made sense that she'd have seen what was going on.

"I sure think so. The cops didn't say anything, other than it was under investigation and they were leaning toward natural causes. They believe she fell from her balcony. At least, that's what Verona told me."

Verona Price was Lemon Bay's Chief of Police. Joss found it highly shocking that Verona would have said anything to Bridget at all. Unless it was to humor her or tide her over for a bit until more information came to light. Everyone in Lemon Bay knew that Bridget liked to talk and didn't mind telling random strangers her life story and everyone else's while she was at it. Just because Verona told her something, didn't mean it was the truth. Officer of the law or not, Verona knew better.

"We don't know the facts yet. It's devastating news. Danielle is a lovely woman and no matter what happened she didn't deserve to be taken so soon. If there is anything I can do to help her family, please, keep me in the loop. I know we weren't that close anymore, but still. I loved her like a sister at one time in my life." Joss reminisced.

"Was," Bridget said.

"Was what?" Joss raised a brow.

"She *was* a lovely woman. I can't imagine what her parents are feeling right now. And Robbie. Oh, my gosh. Robbie. What if he doesn't even know yet? Do you think I should tell him?" Bridget's eyes were wide.

Robbie *was* Danielle's boyfriend. Unless he was listed somewhere as someone to call in case of an emergency, he really may not know what happened yet. If the police thought it was an accident, they may call him, but if Bridget was right and it was murder, it was possible that he'd not yet been notified. Granted Joss and Danielle hadn't been close in recent years, she knew that Danielle's parents weren't fond of Robbie, so they might not have him on their list of people to call. More likely, he was on the top of their list of people that could have killed her if that was really the case. Joss didn't want to get too far ahead of herself. Information that came from Bridget wasn't always accurate, so she would wait until she read the paper or heard more on the news.

"I don't think you should put that weight on your shoulders. Robbie probably already knows and is dealing with some hard things right now. My shift is just about over if you want to chat for a little while longer. We can go to my house or something," Joss offered.

"That sounds really nice. Thanks," Bridget said, wiping her eyes again.

CHAPTER THREE

Joss groaned, responding to the knock on her front door. It was her day off, and she'd been hoping to enjoy it alone. The days that she didn't need to wake up at four am were the best ones as far as she was concerned. Looking at the clock that hung on her pale-gray living room wall, Joss forced herself off of the couch and to the door.

"I brought cheesecake," Tyla said the moment the door opened.

"What are you doing here so early?" Joss asked.

"I said, I brought cheesecake." Tyla passed by, heading straight for the kitchen.

"So, something is wrong then I take it?" Joss asked, knowing her best friend well.

17

"Yes. Well, I don't know. There's probably a killer on the loose but then again, would they really stick around the area, just like, waiting to be caught?" Tyla stood with the door open, staring into the fridge.

"Ummm. Hi, Tyla. It's so good to see you," Joss teased. "What's this about a killer?"

Joss knew that whatever Tyla had to say was most likely going to be accurate. After all, she was dating Austin Price, brother to the Chief of Police in Lemon Bay.

"Get this." Tyla poured herself a glass of milk. "Chocolate syrup?" she asked, eating her cheesecake at the same time.

"In the cabinet to the left," Joss answered, knowing how quickly Tyla could lose her train of thought.

"The minute you called to tell me that Bridget came in, I started trying to figure out a plan for why I needed to see Austin. I stopped at his house this morning after my shift was over to see if he knew anything. I left my favorite book there; in case he ever asks why I showed up out of the blue... Anyway, Verona was there. She left just a few seconds after I got there but right before I left, Austin must have told me four thousand times to be careful. He said to watch my surroundings and to never go anywhere by myself. So, naturally, I came right here."

"He said it was definitely murder?" Joss stress ate, and today was no different. Cheesecake at eight am, yes please.

"Not technically, but he might as well have. You know Verona would never tell little old me what was really going on." She lifted a forkful of the decadent, raspberry pistachio swirl cheesecake to her lips.

Joss could appreciate Tyla's attempt at humor even in a dark situation. Verona and she had never gotten along, not when they were rival ballerinas, not when they were both out for homecoming queen, and most definitely not when Tyla started dating her brother. They had an interesting relationship and were civil for Austin's sake.

"Don't make assumptions then. You sound like Bridget," Joss said matter-of-factly. "When was the last time you heard of a murder in Lemon Bay? I mean, come on. It's a pretty slim chance."

"So, then, Danielle's death was an accident but I

should watch out because that same accident could happen to me, too? Be real, murder is a scary thing, but it's certainly possible. What if it was? What if there really is someone in town that killed her? What if we knew them?" Tyla eyed the last slice of cheesecake.

"Eat it." Joss nudged the box closer. "Okay, so let's be careful then. Let's agree not to go anywhere alone.

Tyla nodded. "Who do you think it was? If it was someone we know, I mean."

Joss tried to ignore the morbidity of the question, but if she were being honest with herself, she had thought about it already. Even before Tyla arrived.

"How do you answer something like that? I've known Danielle for the majority of my life. I know her parents, her boyfriend, her coworkers. It's too hard to just assume it was one of them."

"Speaking of coworkers, you heard she recently got a new job?" Tyla mused.

"Yes. I met her new coworkers the other morning after they worked an overnight at the hospital. They all seemed nice."

"So, you didn't know any of them?" Tyla pressed.

"I know what you're getting at, and I don't know why you are like this. Let the police do what they need to do. Verona will take care of it."

"Fine." Tyla sulked.

Before the talk of murder could take over their day, the women were interrupted by a knock on the door.

"Jeez. What is it with people thinking I want company this early in the day?" Joss joked, looking at her friend before going to the door.

"Hey, Jossy!" Lorraine Prior squealed. "I'd hug ya, but as you can see, my arms are full. Help a lady out?"

Joss took one of the bags from Lorraine and padded back to the kitchen, knowing Lorraine would follow.

"Hey, Tyla! Long time no see." Lorraine snorted.

Lorraine was Luke's wife. And as luck would have it, Joss and Tyla both worked at the Day and Night Diner, so it was a regular family reunion.

"What's up?" Joss asked, watching as Lorraine loaded the contents of the bags into her fridge. If

Lorraine was there and had food, that meant she wanted something.

"I just left the diner." She winked at Tyla. "Great job last night by the way. I hear you guys were busy as all get out. My dear Luke isn't feelin' on the top of his game. I just had a little looksee at the schedule in the back, and I noticed that you are the opener tomorrow, Jossy."

Joss hated it when Lorraine called her that.

"That's right," Joss said.

"We were hopin' that you'd do us just a teensy tiny favor, and open up for Luke." Lorraine clasped her hands.

"I'm already opening," Joss said, knowing what game they were playing. Lorraine was asking her to open the diner on her own. That meant taking care of the opening duties for the front and the back of the house as well as all of the cooking while she waited tables.

"Do ya mind, darlin'?" Lorraine asked, still in the same position.

"How can I say no? You brought me all this glorious food." Joss rolled her eyes and shook her head.

For the last fifteen years, Joss had worked for Luke at the diner. She'd started on a whim. It was a busy Saturday morning, and one of the waitresses at the time hadn't shown up for her shift. Joss had seen how busy everyone was and just decided to get up and help. She'd cleared tables, sat customers when they arrived, and even gotten a few drinks for the waitress that was working. Luke had been so impressed with her that he hired her on the spot. They'd had a love-hate, but mostly fiercely loyal, relationship ever since.

"Did you ask Dina?" Joss wondered.

"No. Luke specifically asked for you," Lorraine admitted.

Of course he did, Joss thought. She never wanted to rock the boat with Dina. She considered herself the manager at the diner, although the title was self-imposed.

"One of these days, Luke is gonna have to learn just how important Joss is to him," Tyla chimed in.

"He knows," Lorraine said. "Trust me, he knows."

CHAPTER FOUR

Joss's arms were full. She'd just cleared a table of five getting it done all in one trip. Over the years she'd mastered the best way to stack the plates, cups, and utensils in the most perfect way so that she'd be able to get everything into the kitchen without falling on her face or dropping everything on a customer. At the Day and Night Diner, trays weren't allowed. If you asked Luke why they weren't allowed, he'd tell you safety reasons. If you asked Joss, it was because Dina, the only other woman at the diner that had been working there as long as her, was unable to carry them and it embarrassed her. So, in order for Dina to save face, she'd begged Luke to ban trays. No one could carry a tray of drinks or a tray of food to a table. Multiple trips back and forth were the only option, so Joss and her coworkers had learned to be creative.

It had been a busy morning, and there were a few times when Joss regretted agreeing to cover for Luke, but she'd made it through. Normally, she'd have to get through another little rush before the next waitress arrived, but speaking of the devil, Dina was on the schedule that day. Dina arrived an hour early to every shift. She'd always come into work dressed in something fancy. Three-inch heels, hair perfectly coifed, something that looked like it came from Prom Night 1993. She never said where she was coming from that she'd needed to be dressed as such, but most everyone that knew her believed she did it for attention. She wanted people to recognize her, and they certainly did.

"Josslyn. Where is Luke?" Dina asked, flipping through her hot-pink, sequined clutch.

"He's not here," Joss said, brushing past her into the kitchen.

Dina stood watching Joss as she removed two slices of thick-cut challah bread and dipped it into the freshly made egg wash for the diner's Strawberry Granola French Toast. Once the slices were warmed, but just before they began to brown, she removed the bread and coated it with granola. It went back to the grill to continue cooking while Joss fished through the fridge for the strawberry cream cheese.

"Dina, do you mind helping out a little? I can't seem to find the cream cheese," Joss said, moving things around.

"Where is Luke?" she asked again.

"He's not here, and neither is the strawberry cream cheese that I need for this order. Can you please make some? Or maybe go out front to check on the customers for me while I make some?" Joss took a breath, digging deep for her patience.

"Oh, gosh. Have you seen how I'm dressed? I'd be mortified to be seen out there like this." Dina put her hand to her chest.

"You just walked in here through the front door, passing everyone on your way into the kitchen," Joss reminded her.

Dina squinted her eyes and let out a huff. "Fine. I'll make it. But then I have to go get changed so I can clean up your mess." She glanced at the dishes in the sink. "And how many times do I have to tell you to write down the orders on the order slips?"

"Thanks," Joss said simply, not looking for a fight. "I appreciate the help."

Dina was, well, she was Dina. She was good at her job, and she was even good at the job she thought she had. Dina aspired to be the manager of the Day and Night Diner and sometimes she'd tell people that she was. She wasn't. Luke never gave her the manager position, in fact, no one was the manager. Sometimes it seemed like he couldn't decide between Dina and Joss, so he just didn't decide at all. The diner never suffered, though. Everyone who worked there went above and beyond to make sure that things were taken care of, especially in Luke's absence.

"Here's your cream cheese. Now let me get changed. I certainly didn't think I'd get here early just to end up working. I thought I'd have a bit of time to change, eat something, and do some catering work." Dina set the bowl of freshly whipped cream cheese mixed with strawberries and a bit of confectionary sugar in front of Joss.

"Thanks, Dina. I'll be fine until it's time for your

shift. Get something to eat. What do you want? I'll make it for you," Joss offered.

"Something healthy. A parfait with extra fruit, and use the cinnamon granola not the almond. Thanks." Dina smiled before stalking off.

She really wasn't that bad of a person. It was her one-sided rivalry with Joss that got in the way of things. Dina knew Joss was the favorite at the diner. Not only did Luke love her and trust her, but she had a bond with the customers that Dina didn't.

Joss finished the French toast, served a handful of other customers, and made sure that in between tasks she got the dishes washed. When Dina was done in the office, Joss wasn't going to let her find a reason to complain. The customers were happy, the kitchen and dining room were clean, and that was all that mattered.

"Here's your parfait," Joss said placing it on the table in front of Dina. "Just how you like it."

The front door creaked open and Ryan Leclair strolled in.

Dina looked up. "Oh, I'm not sitting here. I just was resetting the tables. The salt and pepper shakers were switched. Pepper on the left, salt on the right. Why can't you remember that?" Dina shook her head.

Dina quickly picked up her parfait and rushed to the counter. Ryan always sat in the fourth stool from the cash register and Dina plopped down right beside him just seconds before he reached his spot.

"Hi, Ryan." Dina grinned. "Joss, get him his coff..."

Joss set Ryan's coffee mug down on the counter in front of him before Dina could finish.

"Awww. Look, my favorite mug." Ryan chuckled.

"Whatcha gonna have this morning?" Joss asked, making sure to pull out the order pad from her apron especially for Dina.

Ryan stirred the cream into his coffee and glanced up at the menu board where the daily specials were written every morning. "What about number 3? Two buttermilk pancakes, two eggs over easy and a couple slices of bacon."

"I can make it for you!" Dina hopped up from her stool, shoving her parfait to the side. "I make the best pancakes." She bragged.

"She does make a heckuva pancake," Joss agreed, trying not to laugh at Dina's attempt at flirting.

Ryan and Joss shared a glance. There had always been a bit of attraction between the two of them. For Joss, she felt like mixing work with pleasure wasn't a good idea. She was afraid that if they went out on a date and it didn't work out that it would ruin the diner for Ryan and he wouldn't come back. That never stopped Ryan from asking her out.

"So, how's life?" Ryan asked.

"Good." Joss nodded. "It's been a really busy morning. I covered for Luke and was already scheduled to open so it's been pretty hectic but hey, I guess it makes the day go by faster and that's gotta count for something."

"Is your shift almost over? We should do something," Ryan suggested. "The weather is supposed to be pretty decent this afternoon, we can go out on the boat. It'll be fun."

"I'm working the lunch shift too." Joss felt herself blush. "Maybe some other time."

"Ahhh. The standard answer. Maybe when you get done switching the salt and pepper shakers back, you'll reconsider. Salt on the left, pepper on the right. What kind of monster does it the other way?" Ryan joked.

Joss couldn't help herself. She let out a giggle just in time for Dina to come around the corner from the kitchen.

"I forgot to ask." She eyed Joss. "Did you want your bacon a little crisp this morning?"

"Sure, Dina. That'd be fine," Ryan agreed.

"Better get to work before you get yourself in trouble." Ryan laughed. "But keep that boat ride in the back of your mind. I bet you'll want to relax when you get out of here later."

CHAPTER FIVE

"Thanks for today." Luke rested his hand on Joss's shoulder. "I know it was a long one, and I shouldn't have even asked."

"You didn't." Joss winked. "Lorraine did. I might complain about it every now and then, but the truth is, I like it. Cooking is fun and something that I don't get to do all the time and being busy like I am when I'm the only one here isn't that bad. Everyone is very understanding."

"They shouldn't have to be, though. It's my fault that I just leave you to your own devices so often and I apologize for that. There's just so much going on lately and I'm being pulled in all these different directions. I'm just thankful for you and I wanted to make sure you knew it." Luke gave a single nod and got back to the grill.

Joss didn't need to say anything else. She knew how hard it was for Luke to get those words out and rather than make him feel uncomfortable by getting sappy, she smiled to herself and went out the kitchen door.

Before Joss even reached her apartment building, she saw a vehicle sitting in the visitor's parking spot dedicated to her apartment. The massive, black truck belonged to Bridget who was most likely there to talk about Danielle again. It took everything out of Joss to not keep driving right past her apartment building so she could avoid the situation, but she knew her friend just wanted to talk. She pulled into her spot and got out at the same time Bridget did.

"Sorry to just stop by like this," Bridget said, walking alongside Joss.

"It's no problem. Is everything okay?" Joss frowned, hoping something else hadn't happened.

"I'm okay. I'm just really curious is all. I can't stop thinking about Danielle and who could have done something so awful. She was such a nice person and didn't deserve something so terrible."

"Did you hear something more about it?" Joss asked, wondering what Bridget was thinking.

"Not officially."

Joss wasn't sure what to make of that. "Officially?" she asked.

"Yeah. I didn't talk to the police or anything. I mean, they questioned me since I was her best friend and one of the last people to see her but I was at work, so they aren't really interested in me anymore. But that hasn't stopped me from being interested, if you know what I mean."

"I have no idea what you mean," Joss admitted.

"Aren't you curious? Even a little bit?" Bridget asked once they'd gotten settled inside.

"I haven't spent a ton of time thinking about it honestly. It's sad. We lost a friend, and that's terrible. I don't know what more there is to say." Joss pulled two bottles of water from her fridge and passed one to Bridget.

"I've got a lot to say. Like, how about Robbie..." Bridget paused, sipping her water.

"How about Robbie what?" Joss asked, afraid that she was catching on. What was it with her friends trying to be Nancy Drew?

"Robbie and Danielle had been together forever. They'd been through so much in their relationship including Robbie putting his career on hold so Danielle could go to nursing school."

"That was nice of him. I didn't know that."

"Nice, yes. Motive for murder... Heck yes." Bridget slammed her bottle on the table, splashing it all over.

"Really?" Joss wiped water splatters off her arm.

"Sorry, but Robbie gave up his dream so Danielle could achieve hers. What if he got so upset about that that he took it out on her in the ultimate way?" Bridget prodded.

"What are we doing right now?" Joss asked. "Robbie did not kill Danielle."

"We don't know that. It's completely possible that he

got mad and pushed her off the balcony into the bushes and she was instantly killed. Didn't you hear about all her broken bones? A fall like that could totally kill someone. Plus, they said they found footprints in the dirt by the bushes. They could have been Robbie's."

Joss wanted to freeze time. She needed a few minutes to process what was going on. Bridget, a woman that she'd known rather well at one point in their lives, seemed to be suggesting that they try to solve a murder together. That couldn't be right. Not only was it a one in a million chance for a murder to have occurred in Lemon Bay, but it was their friend who had been killed. Joss understood Bridget's desire to learn the truth, but certainly, that didn't mean they should be the ones investigating. Where on earth would a waitress and a dog walker have gained the skills to do such a ridiculous thing?

"I know what you're thinking," Bridget continued. "But trust me. It's a good idea. All we have to do is ask Robbie a few questions. We can get him talking and try to confuse him or something."

"You think we can get him to admit it? Just like that?"

Joss was incredulous. "The footprints could have been Robbie's because he was dating Danielle and spent a lot of time at her house. Or because he is a landscaper for a living and may have planted those bushes himself. Were they even the footprints of a man?"

"Maybe. Maybe not, but there's only one way to find out. What do you say? Want to come with me? Please?" Bridget begged.

Joss sighed. "Well, I can't very well let you go alone, now can I?"

Bridget jumped from her chair, squealing. "We are gonna figure this out. I just know it!"

"So, what? Robbie is our only suspect?" Joss asked, mentally groaning for even saying that out loud.

"See! You're already interested in it." Bridget paused, frowning. "I just want to say that I don't want to seem insensitive. I realize that I'm probably more excited about this than I should be, but I just can't sit back and wait on the police to follow their procedure and policies and all that. I can't handle the thought that someone killed my best friend and I'm just happy you agreed to help."

"I get it. I just don't want to do anything crazy. I'm going with you so you have backup in case something bad happens. Although, I have to admit, I'm not so sure I think that Robbie could have hurt her. I didn't know him well, but I believe he loved her," Joss said. "It could have been someone else."

"I believe that he loved her too, but I'm not so sure that matters sometimes. Don't you watch movies? You see all these killers and find out that they killed their spouse. It happens, unfortunately. I suppose you're right, though. It could have been anyone."

"Anyone?" Joss asked. "Does that mean Danielle had people that didn't like her or maybe an enemy?"

Joss felt like she had just entered one of those movies Bridget had mentioned. Next she'd be on a stakeout, wearing black clothes and drinking coffee at three am to keep herself awake.

"Enemies?" Bridget winced. "I don't think I'd say that. Not that I know of anyway. I guess Jessica may have been a little upset with her."

"Jessica Stetson?" Joss asked.

"Yeah. When Danielle left the nursing home, Jessica was mad about it," Bridget told her.

"Do you know why?"

"Beats me. I could guess and say it was because Jessica was the one who got her the job at the nursing home."

"Could be another person to talk to then, right?" Joss pointed out.

"You're good at this already!" Bridget said. "When do you want to start and with who? Robbie or Jessica?"

"Tomorrow. It's been a long day," Joss said, hoping that the police would already have the murder solved by then.

In the meantime, Joss was going to read the news and check out the articles online. If she was going to do this, she was going to do it right. She'd search the social media profiles of Danielle, Robbie and Jessica to see what she could find.

"Okay. Let's just be cautious, okay? The last thing we need is Verona finding out," Bridget chided.

The last thing both of them needed was Verona finding out. Joss knew what she was agreeing to probably wasn't the smartest thing she's ever done, but Danielle had been her close friend for many years and while Verona was excellent as the chief of police in Lemon Bay, she had solved just as many murders as Joss had. A grand total of zero. Because zero things like this happened in their town. Until now.

CHAPTER SIX

"Another day, another dollar, huh?" Garth greeted, flipping a burger patty on the grill.

"That's how it goes," Joss agreed, smiling at him through the window that looked into the kitchen.

Garth Myers was the other cook at the diner. He usually worked overnight, but had come in early to learn more about the lunch shift. While the diner was open all hours of the day, the overnight shift was never as busy, or even close, to the lunch shift.

"Tyla, order up!" Garth yelled, letting them know that the food for table 6 was ready to be delivered.

"I'll take it," Joss offered, resting one of the plates on her arm.

Joss carried the four plates over to the table where Tyla met her so she could pass out the food. A little trick of the trade was to never call out the food order. Walking up to the table and asking what dish belonged to who, was something else that wasn't allowed at the diner. If one waitress delivered another waitress's food, it was a rule that you always write down the orders on the slip starting with the person to your left. That way, there was never any confusion for the person delivering the food.

"Enjoy your lunch!" Joss left the table and headed back toward the counter. She needed to fill the ice in the soda machine before the customers started rolling in or she'd have no time to get it done.

Glancing around to make sure none of her tables were in need of anything, she went in the back to the ice machine. Carrying two large five-gallon buckets on her way back to the dining room, she ran right into Ryan.

"Oh, hey," she said, struggling with the full buckets.

"Let me get those," he offered, taking them from her with ease.

"Thanks. They go just over by the..." Joss began.

"I know. I've been coming here a long time and watching you do this.

Joss looked at him funny.

"Well, not watching *you*, but watching how things work." His face turned red.

Joss appreciated the fact that their attraction was mutual as was their awkwardness. Something about feeling like they were still in high school made her giddy and she enjoyed when Ryan came into the diner.

She followed Ryan to the soda machine where she'd expected him to just put the buckets down, but to her surprise he lifted them both up and poured them in for her.

"That was really helpful. Thanks again," Joss said. "Those things are heavy!"

"Put in the turkey club special with fries for me and we'll call it even." Ryan grinned.

"Easy enough," Joss said, getting him his usual lunch beverage, a root beer.

"I was going to say we should go to the hot air

balloon festival this weekend but..." Ryan trailed off, his eyes twinkling.

"Sounds like fun actually, but I'm working," Joss told him.

"Of course you are," he replied.

Joss dropped the order slip for Ryan's lunch off to Garth and began making a few salads for lunch. They made eight salads each day in preparation for a busy shift. Filling half the bowls with romaine and the other half with spring mix, she sprinkled a few onion slices, three cherry tomatoes and, a couple of cucumbers in each bowl. They saved the croutons for just before serving, that way the bread stayed crisp.

"Order up," Garth said again.

Joss grabbed the plate from the window and carried it to Ryan. "Can I get you anything else?" she asked.

"I'm good for now, thanks."

Joss made the rounds to all of her tables, making sure everyone was taken care of. She saw Tyla taking orders for a large group on the other side of the diner, so when the small group of three entered the building, she told them to have a seat where they'd like and she'd be right with them.

When Joss got to the table, she realized who was sitting there. She'd been in a daze, something that happened every time Ryan came in - she should really consider just agreeing to a date - and hadn't recognized that some of the people who had just walked in were the ones that had come in with Danielle the day that she died.

"Good afternoon," Joss said. "What can I get everyone started with?"

The group placed their drink orders and one of the women in the group spoke again, "can we order our food too? We have to be at work for a meeting in an hour."

"Of course." Joss nodded. "Go ahead."

"I'd like a patty melt and fries," the same woman ordered.

"I think we're both going to have a ham and cheese melt with onion rings," the other woman at the table ordered, gesturing to the man next to her.

"Sounds great," Joss said, reaching out for their menus.

Joss handed the order slip off to Garth, got her new table their drinks, checked on Ryan and helped Tyla carry out the appetizers for her large table. Before she knew it, Garth was calling out for her again. She delivered the food to the three people that she couldn't help but be curious about.

"Let me know if you need anything else," Joss said before backing away from the table, her mind reeling with questions she wanted to ask them. She decided that if they were done eating and still had time to get to the hospital before their meeting, she'd dig deep and find the courage to talk to them about Danielle.

Just as she was chickening out, they called her over.

"Lunch was great," one of the women said. "Do you mind getting us to-go cups for our drinks and a box for Jesse's food?"

"Was there something wrong?" Joss asked.

"Oh, no. He just hasn't had much of an appetite lately."

This seemed like reason enough to chime in. "I'm sorry if I'm overstepping but, are you three Danielle Perry's coworkers? I think I remember you coming in with her before."

Jesse cleared his throat and slid out from his chair, leaving the table.

"I'm sorry. I didn't mean to upset anyone." Joss frowned.

"It's okay. I remember you too. Jesse and I have been here with her before. It's such a shame what happened. I'm Maggie and this is Traci. That was Jesse who just left. We all worked with Danielle at the hospital."

"Were you all very close?" Joss asked, hoping she wasn't being too nosy.

"Jesse and Danielle were very close. They even worked their schedules out so they could work the same shifts. I wasn't very close to her, but she was a really nice person. I miss having her around," Maggie said.

Joss looked to Traci. "What about you?"

"I never knew her. I'd been on a leave of absence

when she started at the hospital," Traci admitted, never looking up from the table.

"I grew up with her and I miss her a lot. We weren't as close as we used to be, but friendships like ours never fade away completely," Joss told the women, hoping that offering her own story helped ease them a bit.

"I'm sorry for your loss," Maggie said, getting up from the table. "We hope to see you again, but we have to run. We enjoyed everything. Thanks again."

Traci tossed a few bills onto the table and they left the diner, Joss watching them out the window until they got in a car to leave and even then, she watched them drive away.

CHAPTER SEVEN

Joss and Bridget sat across from one another on Bridget's deck, waiting for Robbie to arrive. They were trying to act casual and hoped it was working.

"It was a really good idea you had to call the lumber yard before we just showed up there looking for Robbie. He probably would have thought we were nuts." Bridget laughed.

"This makes much more sense. We would have gotten to the lumber yard and had no idea what to do with ourselves. Now that Robbie thinks he's coming here to give you an estimate on some land-scaping for around the house, it'll be was easier to have a personal chat with him. We can ease right in and see what we think. Plus, we're at your house, you have a ton of neighbors who all seem to be outside right now working in their own yards."

Joss didn't want to toot her own horn or anything but once she'd vetoed Bridget's plan of just showing up at the lumber yard to see Robbie, she suggested they just drive around town looking for his work truck, hoping to find him that way which also seemed like a terrible idea. Joss thought asking Robbie to come to them was a much better plan.

"Also, I really might use him. For landscaping stuff, I mean. Have you seen my yard? It's awful compared to everyone else's in the neighborhood."

"Here he comes!" Joss said, sipping her lemonade. Her throat was dry, and she felt her anxiety taking ahold of her.

As Robbie slowly pulled his truck alongside the curb in front of Bridget's house, the women watched him in silence. They'd agreed to say nothing about Danielle until the estimate was complete or if he mentioned it first.

Robbie waved as he stepped out of his truck and made the short walk to her deck. "Bridget, hi. Joss, I didn't expect to see you here," he said.

"I just stopped by to visit Bridget, and she told me you were coming. I figured I'd hang out a little so I could say hi. Long time," Joss said, giving him a quick hug.

"So, what are you thinking? Is this more of a cut the grass sort of project or are you thinking of something a little more of a... drastic change..." He looked across the street, taking in all of the perfectly manicured yards.

"I know. They really go crazy around here. Mr. and Mrs. McGuillacutty have a Koi fish pond in the backyard. The Mendez family has what looks like a rainforest in their yard. I'm not sure I can keep up with them!" Bridget played the part well. "I'd like to see what you think. Feel free to take a look around and give me your honest opinion. I don't want to spend a fortune, but I'd like my house to look like it belongs here."

"On it," Robbie said, nodding at the women before heading back to his truck.

The women watched as he walked back toward the house with a clipboard. He was looking up and down, and all around the property. There was no mistaking that he believed he was only there for an estimate. They let him do his thing and about twenty-minutes later, he came sauntering back up to the deck.

"I think we should work on keeping your grass at a decent length first of all. We can add some nice bushes along your side yard and to give it a little more curb appeal, I think some simple flower boxes on your windows would do the trick. What do you think?" Robbie asked, passing the estimate to Bridget.

"Let's get it done. When can you start?" she asked.

Robbie hung his head a moment as if he were thinking about it. "Well, as you know, Danielle's funeral is in a couple of days. I'd really like to try to get through that before I think much about trying to be creative. I've only had estimates scheduled since, well, since you know when. I can't imagine trying to think about what colors match what right now or where I should place things for the best effect."

"I completely understand," Bridget said gently. "I'm sorry I made you come all the way out here. I've been struggling myself lately and just felt like I needed a change."

Joss was impressed with Bridget and how quickly she was able to think on her feet. However, she was probably just telling the truth. Bridget was sad, there was no doubt about that, but the idea of solving her best friends murder was more than enough to keep her busy, rather than sad.

"I'm sorry about Danielle. How are you doing with it all?" Joss asked, pointing to the chair next to hers.

"Not gonna lie, it's been tough. I miss her and I know she's gone, but it doesn't seem real yet, if that makes sense." Robbie sat, leaning back into his chair.

"Perfect sense." Bridget nodded.

"If you need help going through her house or anything, just let us know. We'd be happy to help," Joss offered.

"I think her parents are going to take care of that. Since we didn't live together, we just had a few things at each other's houses. I haven't been brave enough to really look at what she left at my house. I'd rather just leave it there and let it sit. It's a nice reminder of her," Robbie said. "Thanks for the offer though."

"I don't want you to think you have to rush to come

do any work around here or anything, but I would like to hire you," Bridget said.

"Honestly, I'll be putting in my two-weeks notice at the lumber yard soon. I'm going to just do the landscaping and maybe go back to my roots. It's been a long time since I considered working behind a screen, but it's always been my goal," Robbie told them.

"That's right. I forgot you went to school for graphic design. You still think you want to do that?" Joss asked.

"Definitely. Now more than ever. With Danielle gone, I can focus on that without feeling guilty." Robbie paused. "I feel guilty for even saying that, actually."

"Guilty?" Bridget's voice was high-pitched.

Joss gave a light kick of her foot, making contact with Bridget under the table.

"Why would you feel guilty? About your job, you mean?" Joss asked.

"Of course. Danielle worked hard to get into nursing school and I supported that for a really long time. I wanted to make sure she was happy and in order for that to happen, I had to put my life and my career on hold. That meant slinging wood around for contractors all day. I didn't enjoy it but Danielle was happy and so was I. Until she got the job at the hospital, that is. She told me it would be better money and better hours. Only one of those things was true. The money was good and she did really well for herself, but the hours were terrible. When she told me that they were going to be switching shifts at the hospital and all the newcomers were required to work the overnight shift, I didn't really get on board with it, but I didn't have a choice. She wasn't hired to work that shift, yet a couple months later it was a mandatory thing. It just put unnecessary stress on our relationship and I'm not sure how true it really was."

"We get it." Joss nodded, looking at Bridget.

"Well, I better get going. I have another estimate to get to in twenty minutes. I appreciate the call Bridget, and the business. I'll get in touch with you next week."

Robbie went down the few steps to the walkway before Joss squealed.

"Did you hear that?"

"What?" Bridget asked.

"Robbie just said the overnight shift was mandatory, right?"

"Umm, yeah. So?"

"Danielle's friends from the hospital came in to the diner and told me that she and a guy named Jesse adjusted their schedules so they could spend more time together. He seemed really upset about her death too, definitely more so than the others. What do you think that means?" Joss asked, crossing her arms, proud of her realization.

"Danielle wanted to work overnight with another guy?!"

"That's what they said. But, if she told Robbie it was mandatory, we need to figure out who is telling the truth," Joss mused.

"How do we do that?"

"We find someone at the hospital and we ask. It was either mandatory, or it wasn't."

"If it wasn't, then she was lying to Robbie and that might mean much more than the fact that he'd put his own career on hold. You heard him say he wasn't sure if she was being honest about the hours or not. He could have found out that she was lying on top of everything else and snapped."

"Exactly," Joss said. "We have more digging to do."

CHAPTER EIGHT

"Are the Sternos in that box over there?" Joss asked, peering around the catering stockroom.

Tyla looked in the box. "There are seven of them in here, but I don't think that will be enough."

"It's not," Dina said, bounding into the room like she'd been sitting by waiting to be needed. "According to the invoice, we'll have eighteen chafing dishes set out and we need at least two Sternos under each one to help keep the food hot."

"Alright. I can stop off at Restaurant Supply on the way. You can drive the van and I'll follow you in my car," Joss told Tyla.

"Well since no one bothered to order them, I guess that will have to do," Dina said.

"Don't you do the orders?" Tyla asked, resting the box she'd been holding on the edge of a metal shelf.

"Yes," Dina scoffed. "But you two decided you could do this event on your own, so I didn't do any of the ordering. You may have gotten the food and drinks right, but it's all those little details that are important to remember."

"It was one thing and I can buy some at the store. It's not a big deal. Problem solved." Joss sighed and finished packing up the display trays for the desserts.

"Yes. Problem solved. Great job girls," Luke said, entering the stockroom. "How about Dina runs to Restaurant Supply right now so you two can keep packing up. This is a big event and we want to make sure it goes smoothly, right, Dina?"

"Of course we do. I'm on my way." Dina turned on her heel.

Twenty minutes later, Dina had returned with the Sternos, Tyla and Joss had all the food packed up and ready to go, along with all of the utensils, linens, and displays. They piled everything in the catering van and were on their way to Memorial Hall, Lemon

Bay's largest hall and dedicated home to all functions held by locals.

They arrived a bit early, but had wanted time to set everything up before everyone else arrived. To their surprise, they'd apparently arrived entirely too early since there appeared to be a cleaning company there working.

"Did we get the time wrong?" Tyla asked. "Dina would never let us live that down."

Joss looked at her watch. "No. I'm sure we're right on time. Let's go see what's going on."

The women pulled the van into the nearest parking spot and got out, heading toward the hall. They'd have parked closer, in the spot marked for catering vehicles, but the cleaning company seemed to have been confused and parked their own van in the spot.

"Emily wouldn't have parked there," Tyla said, as if she'd read Joss's mind.

"Good point." Joss stopped walking. "Doesn't Emily do the cleaning here?"

"I thought so. Maybe they aren't here to clean. Maybe they are here for the event," Tyla pointed out.

"Maybe." Joss kept walking.

As they go closer to the hall, their questions were answered.

"Howdy, ladies." A man in khaki overalls greeted them. "We'll be out of your hair soon. Just finishing up."

Joss eyed the logo on the van. Suds and Studs. They were a new company in Lemon Bay, run by all men. From what she'd heard about them, they were great, but she couldn't figure out why they were the ones there cleaning when she knew that Emily Rains was the usual person to take care of Memorial Hall.

"Thanks. If you don't mind, we'd like to start getting set up. We won't be in your way, will we?" Joss asked.

"Not at all. Please, do what you need to do. We're just here doing a sample cleaning. Nothing huge. I'm Marlon." He extended a hand.

"Hi, Marlon." Joss shook his hand.

"What's a sample cleaning?" Tyla asked.

Marlon chuckled. "Basically, we come in and show the client what we can do. We make everything shine and give them an example of what it would be like when they hire us."

"Well, good luck with everything. Hopefully you don't have much competition," Joss said, trying to be kind.

She wasn't close with Emily, but she knew that the woman struggled to get business sometimes. As a one woman company, she had a lot to take care of and Joss knew that Emily really relied on the Memorial Hall cleaning job. Hopefully Emily was okay and nothing had happened, causing the town to decide to hire someone else.

"Let's get to work," Joss said, getting back on track. "We can leave the food in the van until the cleaning guys leave so we don't worry about any products getting near the food."

Tyla nodded and opened the back of the van, passing a box to Joss. They made several trips back and forth making sure everything was inside, set up, and ready to go. When the cleaning company left, the women brought in the food, set up the chafing dishes and lit the Sternos to help keep everything hot.

"It looks beautiful," Melinda Markey said, walking across the room, heels clicking as she came closer.

"Thanks!" Joss beamed.

"You do wonderful work. I'll be sure to pass that on to Luke the next time I see him. You ladies are more than welcome to stay and eat with us. I'm sure the department heads of Lemon Bay wouldn't mind a couple of locals joining," Melinda offered.

"I think we have to get back to work, right Joss?" Tyla said.

"She's right. Thanks for the offer. Give us a call when everyone is done, and we can come back over and clean up," Joss said, picking up a few stray napkins.

"Thanks again, you two. It looks great and I'm sure it will be well enjoyed," Melinda said with a wave.

"Time to get back to the real world. This was really fun though. It's been so long since we've done a catering job together. I wish Dina wasn't such a stickler for being in charge of catering. Especially when no one even specifically asks for her and we do the same job she would do," Tyla complained.

"It was fun," Joss agreed. "We should try and do it more often."

"Yeah." Tyla nodded, looking at her phone. "We have a little time, what do you think about making a quick stop before we get back to work?"

"What did you have in mind?" Joss raised a brow.

"Let's go see Emily. She might not be at home, but aren't you a little curious why the hall had another cleaning company here?"

"It crossed my mind, but I didn't think it was something I needed an answer to or anything. I'd rather stop and get a smoothie or something," Joss said, honestly.

"Fine. A smoothie does sound good. Maybe not better than a little gossip, but that's okay. It'll do."

CHAPTER NINE

Joss sipped her iced tea. It was an unusually quiet afternoon at the diner so she decided to use that time to sit and relax. It was Friday and that meant she worked a double. After getting to work just before six am, she'd work until three, take an hour break and come back for the dinner shift. It was typically a great money day, but she was enjoying the quiet for now. She had a lot on her mind, and the thought of the chicken sandwich she'd ordered was making her mouth water.

Tyla wasn't feeling well so Becky had agreed to come in and cover for her. Since there were only three tables in the restaurant with people at them, Becky was more than capable of handling that while Joss ate. She enjoyed her food, taking her time to savor it.

Then, the front door opened. Joss turned to look at who had arrived and quickly shoved a handful of fries in her mouth before dashing into the kitchen. Robbie and Danielle's parents had just walked in and seeing them together had to mean something. The Perry's openly showed their disdain for Robbie and always had. Their issues went back several years. They thought Robbie should have followed their timeline for his relationship with Danielle. They believed he should have proposed to her after she graduated from nursing school, but he'd yet to make that happen. It wasn't until they left Lemon Bay that things calmed down for Danielle having to deal with the animosity between them.

"Do you mind if I take that table?" Joss asked Becky.

"Aren't you eating?" Becky looked confused.

"I'm done," she replied, taking the last fry off her plate.

"Go for it," Becky agreed, making a face.

Joss pulled three menus from the basket by the register and carried them over to table 11.

"Josslyn! We were hoping we'd get to see you," Mrs. Perry said.

"How are you?" Mr. Perry stood from his chair for a quick hug.

The Perry's had been like Joss's second family when she was younger. Maybe even closer than her actual family. With her own parents always working, Joss spent a lot of her childhood at the Perry household. She remembered them fondly and hoped they were well.

"Hi," Joss greeted the table. "It's great to see all of you."

"Hey," Robbie mumbled, sticking his face in the menu.

Joss knew that Robbie probably wasn't enjoying the visit and almost felt bad for the guy. The Perry's were sweet, unless you got on their bad side.

"Can I get you all some drinks while you check out the menu?" Joss asked.

"It looks like the menu hasn't changed since the last time we were here," Mr. Perry mused.

"It hasn't." Joss laughed. "If you know what you want, I can get that now as well."

The group placed their orders and Joss strolled off to

get them what they'd asked for, all the while wondering what they were doing together to begin with. It didn't take any longer to cook their lunch than it did to find out the answer to her question.

"Joss, we were hoping you could weigh in on something for us," Mrs. Perry called from across the diner.

Thankfully it was still pretty quiet.

"What's up?" Joss asked once she's gotten to their table.

"We were just discussing Robbie and Danielle's relationship and wanted to get an outside opinion." Mr. Perry glared at Robbie.

"Wow. Umm." Joss hesitated. "I'm not sure I'm qualified to speak on the topic. I don't really know much about..."

"Nonsense. You are just who we need to solve this little conundrum." Mrs. Perry clasped her fingers. "Robbie here claims that he didn't know that his relationship with Danielle was hanging by a thread."

Robbie sighed, and rested his elbows on the table.

Joss couldn't tell if he was frustrated or just waiting for the drama to ensue.

"I'm really not sure," Joss answered. "Like I said, I'm not familiar with their relationship."

"You must know something. You live here, you see these people all the time. There must have been a rumor somewhere along the lines about it. Robbie says all was well in their corner of the world, yet he won't tell us where he was the night she was killed." Mrs. Perry raised her arms.

"That's enough. If you really must know where I was the night she was killed, fine, I'll tell you. Not that the police knowing isn't good enough since they are the ones that really need that type of information, but that's not going to stop you from doing this." Robbie let out a breath. "I was working. I'd picked up a third job to help pay off Danielle's student loans. I promised Peggy Quintero that I'd do some work around her house, just handyman sort of stuff, and I couldn't bring myself to tell her I wasn't coming."

"Peggy Quintero, the pretty little thing who lives on Oak Street?" Mrs. Perry's voice sounded threatening.

"Why would you have told her you couldn't come?" Joss asked, looking toward Robbie.

"Ohhh, I dunno. How about because I was working three jobs to try and support Danielle? I'd just put her through nursing school, and was trying to buy her a ring while she was out working all hours of the night just to spend time with another man. How do you think I felt when I found that out? You think it made me happy to learn that the woman I loved was seeing someone else?" Robbie wasn't holding back.

"So, you were angry with her then?" Mr. Perry bellowed.

Joss put her hand on his shoulder, sensing he was about to get up from his seat.

"Of course I was angry with her. Wouldn't you have been? Any one of you." Robbie looked around the table. "How could she have done something like that to me? After everything I sacrificed for her!"

Mrs. Perry was in tears, her hands shaking violently. "How could you? She loved you."

Joss tilted her head, confused. "Mrs. Perry. Didn't you just hear Robbie? He said that he was at Peggy's house the night Danielle was killed. You aren't trying to accuse him are you?"

"Of killing my daughter? Not at all. But, I don't believe for one second that he wasn't carrying on with Peggy. Buying Danielle a ring, my butt. That's just an excuse because he thinks that's what we want to hear. Why would he do that if he knew she was seeing someone else?"

"She really was seeing him? The guy from the hospital?" Robbie asked. "I didn't know for sure, I just suspected it, but I loved her. From the moment I met that woman, I loved her. I thought if I bought her a ring and if she really was interested in someone else, that it might make her forget about him."

"I'm not convinced I believe you," Mr. Perry spoke.

"What's that supposed to mean? Call Peggy, do whatever you have to do. I didn't hurt Danielle." Robbie defended himself.

"Like Peggy wouldn't lie for a good lookin' man like you." Mrs. Perry twitched her lips.

"That's enough. All three of you." Joss scoffed. "I think it's time to leave. You're causing a scene and acting like this is an interrogation room. I'm sure the police have done their due diligence and if Robbie says he was at Peggy's helping her, I believe him."

Mr. and Mrs. Perry gawked at Joss. For all the years she'd known them, she'd never been anything less than polite. She knew she wasn't one to talk about not letting the police do their jobs since she'd all but interrogated Robbie herself on a different occasion, but the Perrys were attacking him and making him feel like the love he felt for someone was unrequited. That wasn't fair. He'd lost the love of his life and that had to count for something.

"Fair enough," Mr. Perry said, scooting his chair back.

"Joss." Mrs. Perry glared at her before tossing money on the table for the bill and stomping out the door.

"Robbie," Joss began.

"Don't worry about it," Robbie said, putting some money of his own on the table and brushing past Joss on his way out.

CHAPTER TEN

"Emily?" Joss yelled from her car window.

Emily turned her head and looked toward the street where Joss had parked her car. "Oh, hey."

"What are you doing here? I'm supposed to be meeting Bridget," Joss said once she got closer to the house.

"Same here." Emily nodded. "I just finished up her weekly cleaning and she's got my dog, so I'm waiting here until she gets back."

Bridget was the neighborhood dogwalker in Lemon Bay. She and Emily had a barter system. Bridget helped to socialize Emily's dog, Bailey, while Emily did her cleaning.

"I hope everything's okay. She didn't call," Joss said.

"I'm sure she's fine. The dogs are always a handful and she's always a few minutes late." Emily shrugged. "Have a seat. We can wait together."

"I'd like that. It's been a long while since we've had a chance to talk. How are things going?" Joss asked, settling into a chair on the deck.

"Same old, I guess. Business has been slow lately with the new guy in town." Emily frowned.

Joss assumed she was referring to Suds and Studs, the guys she'd seen at Memorial Hall. She'd been wondering what was going on with that after Tyla had questioned it, but she hadn't gotten a chance to see if Tyla had figured anything out.

"I heard," Joss said simply. "I'm sorry it's been tough. Competition is never fun."

"These guys are no joke. Everyone loves them and whatever they are doing for marketing is just blowing me out of the water. I'm guessing it's the whole male only team that brings them the most business. Suds and Studs. What a name, huh?" Emily huffed.

Joss wanted to tread carefully. "I've seen them around. Hopefully you can keep your clients. You've been so loyal to everyone over the years. I'm sure it'll all work out."

"Just seems like everyone has all these great opportunities and I just kinda float by the wayside, hoping for the best. It's not fair, ya know? As if that wasn't enough, I've got Danielle's parents coming by my house multiple times a day."

"What for?" Joss was incredulous. Surely they weren't accusing Emily, too. She felt really bad for her that she was losing a business she'd worked so hard to build; she didn't need more stress added to that.

"Her dad will stop over asking questions, then her mom will come over a few hours later, then the next day, they show up together. Each time they ask the same questions, like they are trying to catch me in a lie or something. I mean, I get it. I can't imagine what they are going through, but I've told them a hundred times that I didn't see anything. Heck, I didn't even know anything happened until I heard all the commotion and saw the police walking around."

Joss felt bad. She knew the Perrys were difficult, but Emily was right. They were just processing their grief in a different way than most people. Since the police hadn't seemed to have released any more information, or had any leads from what Joss knew, she'd have to see if Tyla could find anything out from Austin.

"Wow. I'm really sorry about everything. I'll send you all the positive vibes I can. If I hear of anyone looking for a housecleaner, I'll be sure to send them your way. As far as Danielle's parents go, maybe you can just try not answering the door?"

"I can't do that. No matter how badly I want to. I know they are just trying to find out what happened to their daughter. If I had people that cared about me like Danielle did, I'd be so happy. She was a lucky woman. A great man, so many friends, job offers galore... I mean, whoever killed her must have had some really good reason to do it." Emily emphasized the last sentence.

"I suppose," Joss said, unsure of what else to say. She knew Danielle had good friends and a loving family, but if she wasn't mistaken, it sounded a little like Emily was jealous of that.

Before Joss was able to continue, Bridget drove up, parking her truck on the street behind Joss's car. Two dogs had their head out the window each fighting for the most space.

"Sorry about that. I can move," Emily said, getting up.

"No problem. I have to go back out anyway." Bridget yelled from the street, grabbing onto the dog's leashes and escorting them out of her truck.

"Bailey!" Emily squealed, reaching out for her little Yorkie. "I missed you!"

"She had a great time at the dog park. She and Ralphie were the talk of the town." Bridget pointed to Tyla's ginormous Great Dane who made Bailey look like a dollhouse miniature.

"Well, your house is spotless and my dog looks worn out. I'd say it was a good day for everyone." Emily took the leash from Bridget. "I'll call about next week. I may have to switch the days around if that's okay. See you ladies later!"

"Sure thing. Thanks!" Bridget waved and turned to Joss. "I'm sorry. I should have called."

"It's okay. I'm actually glad you were late. I got to talk to Emily a little. I thought I was coming over here to give you all this juicy news about Robbie, but I may have something else now." Joss leaned back into her chair, Ralphie at her feet, and dove into everything she'd found out.

"Well then," Bridget said. "I don't even know what to make of any of that. What are you thinking?"

"I kind of believe Robbie. I don't think he did it. I can't say anything on the whole Peggy topic, but I don't think he killed Danielle. I'm not sure I think Emily did it either. I'm probably just grasping at straws trying to figure this all out."

"I guess we have some more digging to do." Bridget sighed.

"Yes. But I already have a plan for that. I saw Martin York at the diner the other day and he agreed to see me and answer some questions." Joss grinned mischievously.

"Who's that?" Bridget asked.

"He works at the hospital in the HR department," Joss said, eyes twinkling.

"How'd you manage that?"

"I used to babysit his kids. We go way back. He doesn't know why I want to talk to him, but I'll be thinking of a really clever way to get some answers."

CHAPTER ELEVEN

Joss walked down a corridor at the hospital, taking in the stark-white walls and flooring. She'd arrived early for her meeting with Martin and was exploring the recently renovated cardiovascular wing. She never knew why, but she was always fascinated by hospitals. Most people she knew hated them, but Joss felt an odd sense of calm while she was there. Something about how the hustle and bustle of things still felt serene and silent. As she strolled, she thought about Danielle and what her life would have been like at the hospital. Rushing from room to room, taking care of patients... and Jesse.

Joss stopped in her tracks, seeing Jesse standing at the end of the corridor. He must have noticed her standing there watching him.

"Joss, was it?" he asked, steps away from her.

"That's right. Hi, Jesse."

Joss wasn't sure why she was so taken back by seeing him there. She knew he worked at the hospital, but it hadn't crossed her mind that she'd see him. Honestly, she wasn't even sure that it mattered. From what she knew, Jesse was potentially the other man in Danielle's life. He'd have had no reason to hurt her, so the stinging anxious sensation that she felt seemed out of place.

"Is there anything I can help you with?" he asked.

"I'm just visiting," Joss said awkwardly, noticing the frown of Jesse's face. "Not a patient. Just the wing. I mean, I'm here to see someone, but I'm early so I just took a walk to explore."

"Okay then." Jesse gave a blank stare. "It's not often that I hear people come exploring, but whatever blows your hair back. Have a nice day." He started to walk away.

"Wait! Maybe you can help me with something. I'm supposed to be meeting an old friend on his lunch break and I was just wondering if you could possibly direct me to his office?"

"I'll do my best. Who are you looking for?" Jesse asked.

"Martin York. He said he worked in..."

"HR. Yeah. I can take you there. Do you mind if I ask what you are meeting him for? Are you getting a job here? I didn't realize you worked in the medical field."

"I don't. Like I said, he's an old friend. I used to babysit his kids, and I just wanted to catch up," Joss explained.

Jesse picked up his pace, stepping in front of Joss. "Listen. I don't know you from a hole in the wall, but if you're here trying to snoop around and find anything out about Danielle, I recommend you don't do that." His brown eyes were wide and angry.

Joss put her hands on her hips. "I don't know what you're talking about. I just told you I was meeting a friend."

Jesse took a step closer to Joss, whispering in her ear. "You'd better be telling the truth. If I find out otherwise, you won't like what happens."

Joss jolted backwards, never breaking eye contact, something her father had taught her.

"And for what it's worth, you're looking in the wrong place. Go after the fool that stuck by her side even though she'd been with me for the last six months. He's the one you need to look into. Finding out your girlfriend is leaving you for another man... Can't tell me that's not reason enough to kill someone. I'd have taken care of him on my own, but I can't lose my career. I'm going places ya know."

Joss wasn't afraid, but the sheer cockiness in Jesse's voice appalled her. She hated when people thought that they could stand on their high horse to prove a point when all the while, they were the one in the wrong. Jesse may not have had a clear reason to kill Danielle, but his mean-streak and mention of taking care of Robbie sure didn't make him look like he was on the good side of the law.

Her thoughts interrupted by a ding on her cell-phone, Joss pulled it from her purse. It was Martin, telling her he was running ahead of schedule and could meet her now. Texting back that she was on her way, Joss carried on in the direction Jesse had begun taking her in.

"Josslyn. It's so good to see you. You look different in your normal people clothes." Martin chuckled.

"Yeah. That apron really adds ten pounds," she joked. "Thanks for meeting me. I really appreciate it."

"Anything I can do to help my kids favorite babysitter."

"I doubt they think of me that way anymore. It's been what... twenty years since I did any babysitting?"

"Time flies." Martin shook his head and gestured for her to have a seat. "So, what's up. What can I do for you?"

"Well, I was just wondering if you could get me any information on a few of the employees here at the hospital." Joss began.

"Hold it right there." Martin held up a hand. "I can't give out any personal information."

"I understand," Joss frowned. "Well," she tried again, "I'm sure you know about the passing of Danielle Perry. I was just hoping you could tell me a little about her job and how she did while she was here. If you remember, she and I were best friends growing up and I just felt like we lost touch. When I heard that she was gone, I just started feeling like I missed time with her."

Martin blinked, just staring at her for a few moments before he replied.

"I remember." He sighed. "Danielle was a lovely woman and was great at her job. She hadn't been here for long, but she had some serious competition to get here and she pushed through and got the job she deserved to have. She even volunteered to work the nightshift which is unheard of. She was a great addition to the team. I was sorry to hear of the tragedy, and I'm sorry for your loss, but I'm not sure there is much more that I can tell you."

"She always wanted to be a nurse here. I remember talking about it with her when we were kids. It was her dream. I didn't know how hard she had to work for it, though. I'm so glad she achieved it before she..." Joss trailed off, not needing to finish.

"She did work hard and you should be proud of her. It was between her and one other candidate. It wasn't an easy choice for her superiors to make, but when they finally decided between Danielle and

Traci, it was a relief. I happened to be in the room when she came in after she received the job offer, she was ecstatic and it showed. Like I said, you should be proud of your friend."

Joss had been honest with everything she'd said. She hadn't admitted before that it wasn't until Danielle died that she realized she'd missed her friend. She should have been there for her during her journey through nursing school and attempts at getting an opportunity for the career she'd wanted all of her life. Joss and Danielle had always been able to share personal things with one another and it was hard for Joss to realize that maybe she could have been there for her in the end. Maybe she'd have been able to solve everything if she'd been a better friend.

"I am proud of her. Danielle was a wonderful woman and I regret us parting ways. Thanks for your time. I'm sorry to have bothered you. I shouldn't have come here thinking you'd be able to offer me anything personal."

Joss and Martin both rose from their seats. A quick parting hug was all Joss could muster before she had to leave his office. He'd said that Danielle had competition for the job and that competition's name was Traci. Joss would be crazy to think that it wasn't the same Traci that she'd met at the diner with Jesse and Maggie. He'd also confirmed that Danielle requested to work the overnight shift. That changed everything.

CHAPTER TWELVE

"What do you think?" Luke asked his staff at the diner.

"I think it sounds great!" Tyla said.

"Me, too," Becky agreed. "When do we get to try it?"

"It's a family recipe. I need to make sure it's perfect," Luke said.

A lot of times when the diner was slow, Luke would play around with old family recipes. He'd gather everyone at table 12, right in front of the fireplace- the most charming part of the building- and tell them what he'd been working on. This time he'd shared a white chicken chili recipe that sounded out of this world and it was just about ready for everyone to try.

"Are you serving it tonight?" Joss asked.

"Depends on how good it tastes." Luke chuckled. "It'll be ready within the next half an hour or so. I'll be in my office if you need me."

Luke had a real office with a desk and a filing cabinet and all the other normal things restaurant owners would need. Luke also had his *office* ,also known as his twenty-five-year-old luxury car. He took his breaks there, he made his phone calls there, even some of his meetings were held in his car depending on who he'd be chatting with. He'd roll the windows down, even in a snowstorm, light up one of his favorite cigars, turn on the radio, and promptly fall asleep. It was a joke at this point how often it happened and how lucky he was that nothing dangerous had occurred from the result of his care-lessness. Everyone at the diner had tried to reason with him at one time or another, but he always said that it was his happy place and eventually, it just became a normal part of the daily routine at the diner. Most people thought Luke was stressed out and used the time in his car to relax. He owned a business, had two grown children, one of which was in and out of trouble more often than not, and the other was in medical school. If you asked Luke, everything was just fine. If you asked his wife, she'd say he needed a vacation.

"I'll be wiping the menus down. Call me when it's ready," Joss said.

"What's going on with you?" Tyla slid in the booth next to her. "I feel like I haven't seen you in forever."

"No kidding. I have so much to tell you but we probably shouldn't talk here."

"Meet me in the back when you're done. We can talk there," Tyla whispered ridiculously loudly.

"Jeez. You'd be a terrible spy," Joss joked, nudging her friend's arm.

"Yeah, yeah. You're just jealous of my skills." Tyla performed a ninja kick, nearly blasting a lavender, polka-dotted pantsuit wearing Dina back out the door she'd just come through.

"What is wrong with you?" Dina shouted, teetering on her high-heeled boots

"What's wrong with me?" Tyla whispered in a much lower voice.

Joss tried not to laugh, jumping from her chair to

Dina's side. "Dina. You look... lovely. Have you just come from a date?" Joss asked.

"Of course I have. Where else would I have gone dressed so formally?" Dina side eyed both women and strutted through the dining room, taking the long way around... twice, before making her way into the back. Ten seconds hadn't passed when she came bursting back into the dining room.

"Silly me. I left my change of clothes in the car. How embarrassing to have to walk through here and be seen like this." Dina waved her arms, causing a scene.

"Bless her heart," an older woman at table 2 said, shaking her head.

Joss and Tyla cracked up laughing.

"Soups on!" Luke yelled from the kitchen.

Tyla and Becky dashed to the kitchen, while Joss, the more level-headed of the bunch, checked on the customers before making her way there. Moments from getting to try the soup that she could smell from across the room, Ryan entered the diner. Dina was still in the back changing out of her polka-dotted monkey suit, so Joss knew that she'd have a second with him before she came charging into the conversation.

Joss glanced at the clock, it was before noon, and that meant Ryan wanted coffee. She poured his cup and set it in front of his favorite stool.

"What'll it be?" Joss asked.

"Number 3. I'm starving today. Add an egg, make 'em scrambled and give me a double order of toast." Ryan rested his hand on his washboard stomach. At least that was how Joss imagined it.

"Coming right up," Luke yelled from the kitchen once again.

"I guess he heard you." Joss laughed.

"How are things?" Ryan asked, elbows on the counter.

"Pretty good. Nothing interesting. Just work, as usual." Joss shrugged.

"That's not what I heard." Ryan's lip twitched.

"Oh?"

Joss had no idea what he could be referring to. She did her best to keep her personal life away from her job, not that her personal life was really very exciting.

"Little birdie said you and your friends were doing some Jessica Fletcher business."

"You know who Jessica Fletcher is?" Joss cackled.

"Nice. Great job avoiding the real topic," Ryan said. "But yes, my mother loves her."

"I'm not sure what you mean." Joss leaned against the counter.

"I heard you were trying to figure out who killed Danielle Perry," Ryan explained.

"And where did you hear that?" Joss asked.

Ryan tilted his head. "You do know Austin and I play cards together, right?"

"Oh. Yeah, I guess I may have heard that before." Joss gave a sly grin. "You can't say anything. Please."

"Are you putting yourselves in danger?" Ryan asked.

"Of course not. We just asked a few questions is all."

Ryan looked at Joss. "I'm serious. It's not safe for you to be running around doing anything involving a murder even if you are *just asking questions*."

"I get it. I promise. We're being careful," Joss said, glad that Ryan was concerned for her.

Ryan continued to look at her but didn't say anything.

"What?" Joss asked, beginning to feel uncomfortable.

"I just wanted to point out that no one asked me any questions," Ryan said matter-of-factly.

Joss looked around her, making sure no one was paying attention to them. "Like what?" she asked.

"I don't know. I just keep hearing from Austin what you, Tyla and Bridget are up to. If Austin is freely talking about it with me, I wonder what his sister knows," Ryan mused.

"So, you don't know anything about the murder?"

"Of course not. I mean, I don't think so anyway, but I'd be glad to chat with you about what I know over dinner." He winked.

Joss grinned. "Someday. Right now, I have some white chicken chili to try."

CHAPTER THIRTEEN

Joss hadn't been able to stop thinking about what Ryan had said about Verona. He was right. She had to talk to Tyla. It wasn't a smart choice for Tyla to even be telling Austin anything since his sister was the chief of police. That was bound to cause problems for everyone involved. Not only that, if Austin was repeating whatever Tyla told him to his friends, there was no way to know who else knew. Joss had been honest when she'd said she really hadn't done anything crazy. No snooping around people's houses and definitely no stakeouts. So even if Verona did find out, there was nothing she could do because Joss hadn't done anything wrong... right?

She sat in her car, waiting for Bridget to show up. They'd both had the day off and agreed to meet at

The Bistro for a quick lunch. It wasn't long before Bridget's diesel truck came thundering into the parking lot. Joss never did understand why Bridget drove such a large vehicle, being just under five-feet-tall, she looked a little silly as far as Joss was concerned.

"Hey, girl! Am I late?" Bridget asked.

"Nope. I'm early." Joss laughed, as she stepped out from her car.

"I can't wait to eat," Bridget said, meeting Joss's pace.

"Me, too. I love the food at the diner, but it'll be a nice change to eat here."

The girls placed their orders at the counter and took the tall, metal stand with the number 28 on it. They brought it to a table outside to enjoy the gentle summer breeze and waited for a waitress to deliver their food.

"So, let's talk about Suds and Studs. And I mean *Studs*. A glorious looking specimen that called himself Mike came by with a business card and some information about the kind of work they do, prices and things like that. I guess they are going door to door looking for business."

Joss shook her head. She could only imagine the conversation between Bridget and Mike. Surely Bridget had entertained him with her shiny personality, but that may not have been a good thing.

"I wonder if they are desperate or just trying to take over the housecleaning market here in Lemon Bay," Joss asked. "I kinda feel bad for Emily. She was pretty much the only one here and now all of a sudden, these guys with their team of cleaners come in and take over. That's not fair to her."

"Well, Mike mentioned that they'd just taken on Colonial Care as clients and you told me the other day on the phone that they were at the hall. And... well, he said they were planning to stop at the restaurant downtown and asked if I had any other suggestions for businesses they could visit."

"Wait," Joss interrupted. "The restaurant downtown, like, the diner?"

"I assume. What do you think Luke will say?" Bridget asked.

"Thankfully, Luke is way too cheap to pay someone else to clean the diner." Joss laughed. "It seems like they are trying to focus on getting businesses as clients rather than homes. Maybe Emily will be alright after all."

"I'm a home and I considered it." Bridget shrugged.

Joss stared, giving her best slow blink, unamused face. "If you fire Emily so a cute boy can clean your house, I swear…"

A server stepped out of the bistro and looked around, likely looking for the stand labeled 28.

"It'll be hard to turn down." Bridget chuckled. "Cute boys can clean my house anytime."

"Are you talking about the new cleaning guys? My Aunt Jessica just had them at her house. I refused to leave her house while they were there. They are seriously so good looking." The waitress, several years younger than them, beamed before setting down their plates of food.

"See? Even she agrees." Bridget stuck out her tongue.

"Can I get you ladies anything else?" the waitress asked.

"We're good!" Joss said.

"Cool. I'm Lisa. If you think of something, just let me know!" She bounded off, back into the bistro.

Between bites, the old friends chatted about murder like it was the most normal thing on the planet.

"I just don't know what to make of it all. It seems like it was either Robbie, who has an alibi, or Jesse, who doesn't really seem to have a reason aside from the fact that he was a super creep."

"Or it was Emily because she was jealous that Danielle had so many opportunities."

"Or Traci, because she was out for the same job as Danielle was and when she didn't get it, she flipped her lid and killed her," Joss offered, knowing she was reaching.

"Or, wait what? Traci," Bridget paused mid-bite. "That name sounds so familiar."

"I told you about her. She was at the diner with Jesse and.."

"Traci O'Dell. It has to be her." Bridget laid down her fork and picked up her phone.

"Who's Traci O'Dell?"

"Is this her?" Bridget asked, showing Joss the phone.

Joss was surprised at the photo. When she'd first met Traci, she told her that she never met Danielle, which Joss believed. When Martin told her that Danielle and Traci were out for the same job, she didn't think much of it. The hospital was big and there was a chance that they'd never met one another but had applied for the same job. But, things were different now. In the photo that Bridget was showing her was Danielle and Traci, standing next to one another, in their nursing school scrubs.

"That's her." Joss nodded. "She said she didn't know her. That she'd never met Danielle."

"She lied." Bridget tossed her phone down, red in the face.

"Who is she?"

"She was Danielle's rival in nursing school. They fought over everything and always seemed to be partnered with one another on all the projects. They were always going back and forth about who had the highest grades and what instructor liked who better. They didn't get along. Not even a little. I don't know what the point of lying about that would be unless she was trying to take the focus off of herself."

"That's surprising news. I think we should try and talk to her. Now that we know she's more involved than we thought, the idea of Robbie or Jesse being killers seem much less likely."

CHAPTER FOURTEEN

"I'm sorry. I know I shouldn't have said anything to Austin, but we've just been learning so many different things about the case and it seemed like Verona really didn't have much to go on. Not like she'd tell me anyway," Tyla apologized.

"The back and forth game that you and Verona play can't involve her finding out that we are doing anything at all," Joss said. "For that matter, it's kinda why I haven't suggested that you and Bridget get together and talk about it. The two of you would totally get us caught."

"Oops." Tyla looked out the window of the diner.

"Oops what?" Joss asked, turning around.

"Let me guess. You asked Bridget to meet us?"

"Yeah, but..."

"We can't do this here. The diner is too populated of a place to talk about murder." Joss shook her head.

"Well, how about she and I talk while you visit with Ryyaannnn." Tyla teased, pointing toward the door.

"This oughta be a fun day," Joss said sarcastically.

While Bridget and Tyla went to the table in the far corner to chat, Joss got Ryan a root beer and stood in front of him at the counter.

"So, I've been thinking..." Ryan paused, sipping his soda.

Before he could continue, Joss heard banging. She looked up toward the door and saw a hand slapping at the door, looking for the handle. She could barely make out the curly, brown-haired man over the stack of dry cleaning bags he held in his hands.

"What is going on today?" Joss asked, running to the door.

"Ugh. Oomph. Oh, thank you for the help," the person replied, knocking the corkboard of business cards off the wall on his way by.

"Umm. Sure. Can I help you with something?" Joss asked.

"I'm dropping these off for a..." He fumbled around the bags, trying to find something.

"Let me guess," Joss said for the second time that day. "Dina Partridge?"

"That's right." He nodded. "Is there a place I can set these down? They're getting kinda heavy." He teetered like Dina had in her fancy stilt boots.

"How about the office?" Joss suggested.

"Is there grease in there?" he asked.

Was it April Fools Day? The Twilight Zone? What was going on?

"I'm sorry, what?" Joss scrunched her nose.

"Dina specifically requested that I not put her things anywhere near grease, soda, dairy, or anything that could become sticky. Oh, and avocados. She said to stay away from them, too."

"Of course. What was I thinking? The office will be fine. It's down that hall to the right." Joss pointed.

She made her way back to the counter, still reeling from the odd situation.

"What was that all about?" Ryan asked. "How did you know they were Dina's?"

"Who else would have the dry cleaners drop off their clothes at a diner? The lime green tulle sticking out from one of the bags tipped me off too. I don't know anyone else that would wear that."

"She's a real gem, huh?" Ryan joked.

"She really is. I can't even imagine where she goes to wear those outfits and how on earth she affords to have them all dry cleaned. I don't think, in all the years that I've known her, I've ever seen her wear the same thing twice."

"While you're doing your digging around, you should find out more about her. You've known her for a lot of years, but never thought to ask?" Ryan pointed out.

In the beginning, Joss had tried getting close to Dina and asking her more about herself, but she'd been standoffish, so Joss had eventually just given up. Maybe Ryan was right. She should try again.

"I agree. I shouldn't discount her because she dresses like she's coming from Cinderella's Ball. I'll give it a shot and get back to you," Joss said with a grin. "So, what's for breakfast?"

Joss put in Ryan's order and walked by Bridget and Tyla's table several times to make sure they were staying quiet. Every time she passed by them they weren't discussing the murder, they were talking about the people in Lemon Bay, the upcoming town picnic, and stuff from back when they were younger. It made her sad to think that the only reason people were talking and getting close to one another again was because Danielle had died. Like Ryan said, she should get to know Dina better. She'd hate to go through life not knowing a thing about a person she'd worked alongside of for years.

Joss had realized a lot of things lately and she wanted to make sure she didn't miss any opportunities.

"Hot sauce?" Joss asked, placing Ryan's plate on the counter.

"No thanks. This looks great. Luke's on his game today," Ryan said.

"What do you mean today?" Luke yelled from the kitchen.

Ryan and Joss laughed, forgetting about Luke's impeccable hearing.

"Let me get you a refill," Joss said, grabbing Ryan's cup.

She brought it back and stood still, watching him.

"What's happening right now?" Ryan asked, raising a brow.

"Nothing. I'm sorry. I'm making it weird." Joss turned around to brew more coffee.

"Making what weird?" Ryan asked.

Joss sighed. "Do you want to go out to dinner with me tonight?"

"Will you turn around?" Ryan laughed.

Joss turned around, hoping her face wasn't as red as it felt.

"I would love to go out to dinner with you," Ryan said the moment he saw her face.

"Took you long enough," Joss teased.

"I'll pick you up at seven," Ryan told her just as a large group walked in the door.

Tyla rose from her seat, going to help the customers but Joss raced toward her, glaring the *best friend, please know what I'm trying to tell you* glare, and said, "I've got it."

Joss pushed a couple of tables together and made sure the group was comfortable. She took their drink order and became laser focused on them in order to avoid Ryan. She was glad she found the courage to ask him out, but was so nervous she could barely stand herself.

"You two are finally gonna get together, huh? Gotta say, you surprised me. Never woulda thought you'd be the one to ask him out," Luke said, as if he could read her mind. "Way to go, Joss. I can't wait to tell Lorraine."

She really should try to be quieter when she was at work. And there she was, worried about Tyla and Bridget.

CHAPTER FIFTEEN

"So, how painful has it been?" Ryan asked.

"Painful?" Joss folded her napkin in her lap.

"I've been asking you out for a year. I was walking the line between cute romantic comedy and creepy stalker. Now that we're here, was it really that bad?"

Joss laughed. "You weren't ever creepy. I always wanted to say yes, but I really didn't like the thought of mixing work with my personal life. What if it didn't work out, and you never came back to the diner?"

"I'm not fourteen. Things don't work out all the time, but I hate to waste time and regret years down the road that I didn't try something I wanted to."

"That seems to be a trend around here lately," Joss mused. "That's kind of why we're here. I didn't want to wonder either."

"Does this have to do with Danielle?" Ryan asked.

Joss didn't want to make it weird and admit that the reason she asked him out was because her friend had been murdered, but it was the truth. Sometimes it took something bad to happen in order for people to realize how important friendships and relationships were.

"Sort of. I mean, it's been a long time coming. I've always wanted to say yes." Joss felt herself blushing.

"Change of subject," Ryan said, clearly sensing her discomfort. "Tell me about Danielle."

Joss cleared her throat. "Uh. Well, she and I were best friends growing up."

"I mean about what you, Bridget and Tyla are doing."

"I'm not sure that's a good idea. We don't really know anything."

Ryan tilted his head. "You guys haven't thought about who killed her at all?"

"Of course we have, but that doesn't mean we have any answers. Clearly, we're on the same page as the police, because it's been all hush hush since it happened. I don't like the thought of a killer running around Lemon Bay, I don't like the idea that it may be someone that I know, someone close to Danielle who claimed they loved her."

"So, then you think it was Robbie?" Ryan asked.

"Not necessarily. He said he has an alibi and that there's someone that can back it up. I don't see any reason not to believe that. That means he'd have to have gotten Peggy to lie for him and that involves too many people."

"Peggy." Ryan guffawed. "You mean Peggy Quintero?"

"Yes." Joss nodded. "He was doing some work for her the night Danielle was pushed off her balcony."

"And, did you ever think it was odd that he was there at night?"

"Not really," Joss admitted.

"Okay. Did you ever think about how whoever

pushed her off the balcony got inside her house? It had to have been someone she knew and trusted."

"That's true," Joss agreed. "That describes Robbie."

"And Peggy has been after Robbie for years. She'd absolutely lie for him, even if it meant getting herself in trouble."

"Wow."

Joss was surprised to hear that. She'd never lie for anyone if it meant she was giving someone an alibi for murder.

"I think there's a lot more to this than you realize. I'm sure Verona has gone over all of these things already, too. According to Austin, she has some leads and is actively pursuing them. I think the police are close and I think you should let them handle it."

"I get that. But, since you have answers for Robbie, what about Jesse? Danielle would have trusted him too."

"Who's Jesse?"

"A guy she worked with at the hospital. Apparently she was lying to Robbie about working overnight hours so she could spend more time with him. So, not that two wrongs make a right, but if Robbie was seeing Peggy..." Joss paused, not wanting to condone cheating.

"What does this Jesse guy look like?" Ryan asked.

"Average height, light brown hair." Joss thought back.

"I wonder if it's the same Jesse I'm thinking of. One of the guys I play cards with brought along his cousin, Jesse, one night. He was a terrible card player, but he said he worked at the hospital and kept bragging about one of his coworkers and how she was leaving her relationship to be with him. Seems to me that if I'm right and it's the same guy, he has a pretty decent motive. He was positive that she was leaving her boyfriend for him. If that was Danielle, and she didn't leave Robbie..."

"I met Jesse twice. The first time he rushed out of the diner at the first mention of Danielle. He was there with two other women from the hospital. The second time, he threatened me and said that I was snooping around for answers about Danielle and that I should stop."

"Joss! You said you weren't doing anything danger-ous!" Ryan looked serious.

"I didn't think I was."

"You got into it with someone that could have killed your friend. I'd say that's pretty dangerous."

"We were in the middle of the hospital and if I'm being honest, I didn't think it was him who did it. I still don't. I don't think it was Robbie either. I've been leaning toward it being a woman named Traci. They were rivals in nursing school and were both trying to get the same job at the hospital. Traci lied and said she'd never even met Danielle, but Bridget showed me a picture of them from nursing school. I think she was jealous of Danielle, then angry that Danielle got the job over her. She said she'd taken a leave of absence right when Danielle started at the hospital, so maybe she didn't want to work closely with her, took some time off, and plotted her death."

"Jeez." Ryan rubbed his hands together. "Have you gone to the police with any of this?"

"No. It's all just hearsay, isn't it?"

"I'm not so sure. This Traci person might be a little more than that. I think you should talk to Verona."

"I will," Joss agreed. "You're right. Boy, now I'm really glad that we went out. We may have just solved a murder."

CHAPTER SIXTEEN

"Thanks for covering for me," Joss told Tyla.

"Sure thing! Wouldn't I be an accomplice or something if I refused and didn't let you go to the police with the information you have?"

"I don't think it works that way, and I don't even know if what I have to say is important. But in case it is, I'm going to get it done. I'll feel so much better if I just tell Verona, or whoever is in charge, what I think has been going on. If I'm wrong, well, I can just hope that they get it figured out soon."

"Call me, or stop by here the minute you leave. I'm really interested in seeing how it goes." Tyla dropped some change into the cash register.

"Bridget said the same thing. How about we make a

plan to all meet at my house later? I could use the rest of the day to run some errands and get things done. I'll text Bridget and you guys can come over at like three?" Joss suggested.

"Fiiine. Nothing like making a person wait." Tyla groaned.

As Joss left the diner, she saw the Suds and Studs van pulling into the parking spot next to hers. She lifted her phone to hear ear, pretending she was busily chatting away.

"Joss? Josslyn Rockwell?" A man called out the window.

Joss carried on with her pretend call.

"Ma'am. I just want to talk." The man got out of the van. "I got your name from a woman at Memorial Hall. Please."

"I don't need anyone to clean my house," Joss said as politely as she could.

"That's not what this is about."

"We don't need anyone at the diner either." Joss wanted to do all she could to make sure Emily didn't lose any more business to these guys.

"I understand." The man held up his hands. "But again, that's not why I'm here. I'm Mike, and I just thought we could talk for a second. I think I know something that might be able to help you."

"Okay, Mike." Joss put her phone away. "What exactly do you think you can help me with?"

"First, I'm just wondering why you have so much hostility right now," Mike asked.

"Fair enough," Joss agreed. There was no way this guy would know she was friends with Emily so she explained her issue.

"I apologize. We don't mean to take business away from anyone. We're a small business too, and I believe we should all support one another. I'll have my boss contact her right away."

Joss looked at him, trying to gage if he was telling the truth.

"What do you think you can help me with?" she asked.

"I heard that you have been looking into a murder that happened in town not too long ago." Mike lowered his voice. "I think I might know something."

The irony wasn't lost on Joss. "If you know some-thing, shouldn't you go to the police?" she asked.

"I don't really want to be involved. I thought if I just told you, that you could take care of it and do what-ever it is that you do."

"I'm a waitress. That's what I do. I have no idea what you are talking about." Joss opened her car door.

"Wait! Just hear me out."

"Why don't you want to be involved? If you think you know something about a murder, you shouldn't be afraid of that. What if it helps?"

"I was in trouble with the law a few times in my past and I just don't want to, alright?" Mike huffed. "If you don't want to hear it then fine, I'm leaving."

Joss sighed. "Alright. What is it?"

"As you know, I clean for a living. Sometimes we have some interesting clients. We have one that's fairly new, and she's definitely interesting. She requested that we sign a non-disclosure agreement because of her job, like, in case we see something we shouldn't about her patients I guess. I don't know, but we signed it, and I guess I've just been afraid to say anything until now. Anyway, I knew about the murder that had happened, but didn't know a lot about it. The news hasn't really shared a lot of information with the public. But it was like a sign, I was cleaning up her laundry room and I saw a pile of clothing tucked between the wall and the washing machine. I pulled it out, prepared to do her laundry, and noticed leaves and twigs and little pink and purple flower petals all over her clothes. There were shoes full of dirt, and gloves with yellow pollen looking stuff all over them too."

"Okayyyyy. I don't follow," Joss said. "What was the sign?"

"I threw the clothes in the wash and finished up at her house. I got my payment from her and went to the van, started it and turned on the radio like usual and the first thing I heard was something about the murder. It sparked a thought, so I looked online and found the write-up about the murder. They said she was found in her bushes and there were footprints."

"And you think that the things you found belonged to her because they were covered in dirt and tree remnants?" Joss asked, wanting to clarify.

"It's possible, isn't it?"

"Anything is possible," she said, discounting his story.

"It's obvious you don't believe me and think I'm crazy or something, but I thought it was worth mentioning. If it matters, my client's name is Jessica Stetson."

"I'm sorry. It's not that I don't believe you. It's just a lot of information with little proof, especially since you washed the clothes and she could have been gardening and gotten dirty. Thanks for the information, I appreciate you being honest."

Joss ran everything through her mind that had happened since Danielle was killed. Jessica Stetson had been Danielle's mentor. They'd worked together at the nursing home for years. Danielle was found in the bushes below her balcony and according to Mike, Jessica's clothes were covered in things that could have potentially come from said bushes.

There was only one thing left for her to do.

Joss pulled out her phone and called Bridget.

"Quick, what kind of bushes did Danielle have?"

"Bushes? What?" Bridget asked.

"Under her balcony. What kind of bushes were there?" Joss asked again.

"Azaleas I think, why?" Bridget said, confused.

"K. Thanks. Bye." Joss hung up the phone and opened the Internet browser on her phone.

Azaleas were pink and purple. Maybe Mike had been right. Now, she just needed to figure out why Jessica would have wanted to kill Danielle.

CHAPTER SEVENTEEN

Joss knew her next stop should be the police station to talk to Verona but something told her she could get Jessica to talk. As she sat in her car, still in the diner parking lot, she weighed her options. Taking a deep breath, she pulled her car out of the lot and drove directly to Jessica's house. She was taking a chance that she'd be there and not at work, but trying something was better than doing nothing.

As Joss drive down Jessica's street, she came to a halt. There were police cruisers all up and down the street right in front of Jessica's house. She attempted to turn into a driveway to get herself turned around when she spotted Verona heading in her direction with her hand held up high.

Joss put her car in park and waited for Verona who was gesturing for her to roll down her window.

"Well, well. Josslyn, what are you doing here?" Verona's look was fierce.

"I um. I was just passing by."

"Sure you were. Just because I didn't catch wind of you and your little escapades, doesn't mean you're as good as I am. I'm the police. You may have thought you were one step ahead, but I was walking right along next to you. Only difference is though, this is my job, this is what I do. Get yourself out of here and out of my investigation." Verona turned around and walked off, back toward Jessica's yard.

Did that mean Jessica was the killer? How had Verona found out? Joss could only hope that Mike had found the courage to go to the police on his own after she sort of brushed his story to the side. Before Joss pulled away, she saw Jessica being led out her front door, handcuffed and placed inside a police cruiser. Torn between feeling like she was a minute too slow to solve the crime and guilty that she didn't go to the police sooner, Joss couldn't help but feel a little proud of herself. She'd drawn the same conclusions that the police had. Danielle's killer would be brought to justice and that was the important thing.

Joss drove the fifteen minutes back to the diner, now able to forgo the police station. She still wanted to enjoy the rest of her day off, but needed to be around people she cared about while she did it. Her closest friends worked at the diner and if that meant she needed to sit at work to be with them, then that's exactly what she'd do.

"What are you doing here? What happened?" Tyla pulled Joss by the arm into the office.

Joss relayed everything that had gone on and flopped down in Luke's chair. "Ugh. What a crazy day, huh?"

"Are you kidding? It was a great day! We have to call Bridget." Tyla dug around in her apron for her phone and dialed a number.

"I need to stay busy. What can I do to help?" Joss asked.

"Go home. Take a nap, eat some cake. Celebrate. You solved a murder!" Tyla squealed.

"I didn't. I still don't know why Jessica would kill

Danielle."

"*Jessica killed Danielle?*" A voice came through the speaker on Tyla's phone.

"Apparently," Joss said, repeating the story to Bridget.

"*I know why.*"

Joss was startled. "Why?" she and Tyla asked in unison.

"*I can't believe this didn't click from the beginning. Jessica was Danielle's mentor. She got her the job at the nursing home and when Danielle first started there, she wasn't very good at her job. She kept making careless errors and Jessica vouched for her every single time. I remember listening to Danielle complain about the early days at the nursing home. No one knew why, but Jessica really stuck her neck out for Danielle. When Danielle applied for the job at the hospital, Jessica was probably offended. She'd worked so hard to teach Danielle and then she just left.*"

"So, she felt betrayed and she killed her. Who would have guessed?" Tyla shook her head.

"Suds and Studs." Joss chuckled, explaining that story as well.

"Speaking of them, Emily just left here from picking up her dog. She told me that some guy from there called her and apologized, asking to meet and to see if there was a way they could work something out so they could both share the business in Lemon Bay."

"I still can't get over why there are people fighting over who gets to do the most cleaning." Joss snorted.

"I should call Danielle's parents. I'm sure they already know, but it'll be nice for them to hear a familiar voice. I'm going to encourage them to talk with Robbie. He loved Danielle, and I don't believe for a minute that he had anything going on with Peggy Quintero. Anyway, thanks for helping me out with this stuff Joss, I know getting involved was probably the last thing you wanted to do. And now I know, I never want to do it again. I'll leave the police work up to the police. I'll talk to you guys later."

"Anything for a friend," Joss said, realizing that while it had been a lot of years, Bridget truly was her friend.

Tyla hung up her phone and looked at Joss. "I totally want to do this again. I mean, I hope there isn't another murder but if there is..."

Joss stood up, choosing to ignore Tyla. She could only hope there wasn't another murder in Lemon Bay anytime soon. Joss took three steps before tripping and catching herself.

"What are you two doing in here?" Dina's shrill voice interrupted them.

"What is this thing?" Joss asked, kicking what she'd tripped over.

"Don't do that!" Dina was horrified. "That's mine!"

"Okay, but what is it?" Tyla asked, looking at Dina.

"The finest shoe rack I've ever seen," Dina smiled at the rack. "She's a real beaut, ain't she? I saw her sitting on the side of the road for free... Can you believe that? Free. I passed her by and turned around faster than a hot knife through butter. They don't make 'em like this anymore. My shoes needed the best, and this is it."

"It's lovely, Dina," Joss said. "Hey, maybe we could talk more about it sometime. Over lunch or something."

Tyla was gawking at them both.

"With me? You want to have lunch with me?"

Dina asked.

"Sure. That's what friends do, right?"

"Yes. That's what friends do." Dina lifted her lip into a half-smile. "By the way, Ryan's out front and I think he'd like to see you."

Joss knew Dina had a thing for Ryan, and she appreciated her for saying that. This could be the beginning of a beautiful new friendship. And even more exciting was the potential of a beautiful new relationship with Ryan.

"Hey, you," Joss said, sitting next to Ryan's favorite stool.

"You're on the wrong side." Ryan grinned.

"I'm just visiting. I'm off today," Joss explained.

"Well, I'm glad you're here because you always work today and that's why I came in. I was hoping we could make plans for a second date."

"How about we eat together right now and make plans for a third date?" Joss leaned over, gently bumping his arm.

"I like the sound of that."

ALSO BY GRETCHEN ALLEN

Sundae Afternoon Series

Book 1: Triple Dipped Murder

Book 2: Melt Down Murder

Book 3: A Twist of Murder

Book 4: Caked in Murder

Book 5: Shivers of Murder

Book 6: A Flurry of Murder

The Cozy Tales of a Professional Mermaid

Book 1: Criminals and Coral

Holly and Evergreen

Book 1: The Final Sleigh

AUTHOR'S NOTE

I'd love to hear your thoughts on my books, the storylines, and anything else that you'd like to comment on—reader feedback is very important to me. My contact information, along with some other helpful links, is listed on the next page. If you'd like to be on my list of "folks to contact" with updates, release and sales notifications, etc.... just shoot me an email and let me know. Thanks for reading!

Also...

... if you're looking for more great reads, I am proud to announce that Summer Prescott Books publishes several popular series by Cozy authors Summer Prescott and Patti Benning, as well as Allyssa Mirry, Blair Merrin, Susie Gayle and more!

CONTACT SUMMER PRESCOTT BOOKS PUBLISHING

Follow Gretchen on Facebook!

Twitter: @summerprescott1

Blog and Book Catalog: http://summerprescottbooks.com

Email: summer.prescott.cozies@gmail.com

And...look up The Summer Prescott Fan Page and Summer Prescott Publishing Page on Facebook – let's be friends!

To download a free book, and sign up for our fun and exciting newsletter, which will give you opportunities to win prizes and swag, enter contests, and be the first to know about New Releases, click here: http://summerprescottbooks.com